Welcome to Mind Alcove - A Safe Space For Your Mind.

This self-care journal is designed to be a comforting and encouraging space for your daily self-reflection and growth.

It is designed to:

- Be repetitive to build a habit.

- Focus on your inner thoughts and emotions.

- Encourage deep thinking.

- Let your mind wander and self-explore.

- Capture daily affirmations.

- Help you look back on your journey.

- Be quick and easy to use.

- Track your mood.

Each page is a fresh start. Make it your own and pen down your thoughts & feelings as they are- completely unfiltered. Dedicate a few minutes to reflect upon your day, whenever you want.

Remember: This is your space. A place free from judgement. So don't hold back and set yourself free!

How I feel right now:

Amazing

Good

Okay

Bad

Terrible

My thoughts:

My affirmations for the day:

-
-
-

Today I am grateful for:

-
-
-
-
-

Access Journals &
More Self-Care Tools
On Our App

Scan to download!

How I feel right now:

My thoughts:

My affirmations for the day:

-
-
-

Today I am grateful for:

-
-
-
-
-

Access Affirmation Cards & More Self-Care Tools On Our App

Scan to download!

How I feel right now:

__ / __ / ____

Amazing

Good

Okay

Bad

Terrible

My thoughts:

My affirmations for the day:

-
-
-

Today I am grateful for:

-
-
-
-
-

Access Community &
More Self-Care Tools
On Our App

Scan to download!

How I feel right now:

My thoughts:

My affirmations for the day:

-
-
-

Today I am grateful for:

-
-
-
-
-

Access Breathing
Exercises & More
Self-Care Tools On Our

Scan to download!

How I feel right now: __/__/____

My thoughts:

My affirmations for the day:

-
-
-

Today I am grateful for:

-
-
-
-
-

Access Journals &
More Self-Care Tools
On Our App

Scan to download!

How I feel right now:

My thoughts:

My affirmations for the day:

-
-
-

Today I am grateful for:

-
-
-
-
-

Access Affirmation Cards & More Self-Care Tools On Our App

Scan to download!

How I feel right now:

My thoughts:

My affirmations for the day:

-
-
-

Today I am grateful for:

-
-
-
-
-

Access Community &
More Self-Care Tools
On Our App

Scan to download!

How I feel right now:

My thoughts:

My affirmations for the day:

-
-
-

Today I am grateful for:

-
-
-
-
-

Access Breathing
Exercises & More
Self-Care Tools On Our

Scan to download!

How I feel right now:

__ / __ / ____

Amazing   Good   Okay   Bad   Terrible

My thoughts:

My affirmations for the day:

-
-
-

Today I am grateful for:

-
-
-
-
-

Access Journals &
More Self-Care Tools
On Our App

Scan to download!

My thoughts:

My affirmations for the day:

-
-
-

Today I am grateful for:

-
-
-
-
-

Access Affirmation
Cards & More Self-Care
Tools On Our App

Scan to download!

How I feel right now:

My thoughts:

My affirmations for the day:

-
-
-

Today I am grateful for:

-
-
-
-
-

Access Breathing
Exercises & More
Self-Care Tools On Our

Scan to download!

How I feel right now:

__/__/____

Amazing Good Okay Bad Terrible

My thoughts:

My affirmations for the day:

-
-
-

Today I am grateful for:

-
-
-
-
-

Access Journals &
More Self-Care Tools
On Our App

Scan to download!

__/__/____

How I feel right now:

 Amazing

 Good

 Okay

 Bad

 Terrible

My thoughts:

My affirmations for the day:

-
-
-

Today I am grateful for:

-
-
-
-
-

Access Affirmation Cards & More Self-Care Tools On Our App

Scan to download!

How I feel right now:

__ / __ / ____

 Amazing
 Good
 Okay
 Bad
 Terrible

My thoughts:

My affirmations for the day:

-
-
-

Today I am grateful for:

-
-
-
-
-

Access Community &
More Self-Care Tools
On Our App

Scan to download!

How I feel right now:

My thoughts:

My affirmations for the day:

- ....
- ....
- ....

Today I am grateful for:

- ....
- ....
- ....
- ....
- ....

Access Breathing
Exercises & More
Self-Care Tools On Our

Scan to download!

__ / __ / ____

How I feel right now:

| Amazing | Good | Okay | Bad | Terrible |

My thoughts:

My affirmations for the day:

-
-
-

Today I am grateful for:

-
-
-
-
-

Access Affirmation
Cards & More Self-Care
Tools On Our App

Scan to download!

How I feel right now:

Amazing

Good

Okay

Bad

Terrible

My thoughts:

Consistency shines through, keep it up!

My affirmations for the day:

- ....
- ....
- ....

Today I am grateful for:

- ....
- ....
- ....
- ....
- ....

Access Breathing
Exercises & More
Self-Care Tools On Our

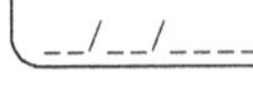

Scan to download!

How I feel right now:

 Amazing
 Good
 Okay
 Bad
 Terrible

My thoughts:

My affirmations for the day:

-
-
-

Today I am grateful for:

-
-
-
-
-

Access Journals &
More Self-Care Tools
On Our App

Scan to download!

How I feel right now:

Amazing	Good	Okay	Bad	Terrible

My thoughts:

My affirmations for the day:

-
-
-

Today I am grateful for:

-
-
-
-
-

Access Affirmation
Cards & More Self-Care
Tools On Our App

Scan to download!

__/__/____

How I feel right now:

Amazing

Good

Okay

Bad

Terrible

My thoughts:

My affirmations for the day:

-
-
-

Today I am grateful for:

-
-
-
-
-

Access Community &
More Self-Care Tools
On Our App

Scan to download!

How I feel right now:

My thoughts:

My affirmations for the day:

-
-
-

Today I am grateful for:

-
-
-
-
-

Access Breathing
Exercises & More
Self-Care Tools On Our

Scan to download!

How I feel right now:

Amazing

Good

Okay

Bad

Terrible

My thoughts:

My affirmations for the day:

-
-
-

Today I am grateful for:

-
-
-
-
-

Access Journals &
More Self-Care Tools
On Our App

Scan to download!

How I feel right now:

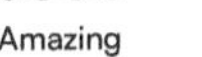
Amazing

Good

Okay

Bad

Terrible

My thoughts:

My affirmations for the day:

- ....
- ....
- ....

Today I am grateful for:

- ....
- ....
- ....
- ....
- ....

Access Affirmation
Cards & More Self-Care
Tools On Our App

Scan to download!

How I feel right now:

 Amazing

 Good

 Okay

 Bad

 Terrible

My thoughts:

My affirmations for the day:

- ....
- ....
- ....

Today I am grateful for:

- ....
- ....
- ....
- ....
- ....

Access Community &
More Self-Care Tools
On Our App

Scan to download!

How I feel right now:

__/__/____

My thoughts:

My affirmations for the day:

-
-
-

Today I am grateful for:

-
-
-
-
-

Access Breathing Exercises & More Self-Care Tools On Our

Scan to download!

How I feel right now:

My thoughts:

My affirmations for the day:

-
-
-

Today I am grateful for:

-
-
-
-
-

Access Journals &
More Self-Care Tools
On Our App

Scan to download!

How I feel right now:

Amazing

Good

Okay

Bad

Terrible

My thoughts:

My affirmations for the day:

-
-
-

Today I am grateful for:

-
-
-
-
-

Access Affirmation Cards & More Self-Care Tools On Our App

Scan to download!

How I feel right now:

 Amazing

 Good

Okay

 Bad

 Terrible

My thoughts:

My affirmations for the day:

-
-
-

Today I am grateful for:

-
-
-
-
-

Access Community &
More Self-Care Tools
On Our App

Scan to download!

How I feel right now:

Amazing

Good

Okay

Bad

Terrible

My thoughts:

My affirmations for the day:

- ....
- ....
- ....

Today I am grateful for:

- ....
- ....
- ....
- ....
- ....

Access Breathing
Exercises & More
Self-Care Tools On Our

Scan to download!

How I feel right now:

Amazing

Good

Okay

Bad

Terrible

My thoughts:

My affirmations for the day:

-
-
-

Today I am grateful for:

-
-
-
-
-

Access Journals &
More Self-Care Tools
On Our App

Scan to download!

How I feel right now:

Amazing

Good

Okay

Bad

Terrible

My thoughts:

My affirmations for the day:

-
-
-

Today I am grateful for:

-
-
-
-
-

Access Breathing
Exercises & More
Self-Care Tools On Our

Scan to download!

__/__/____

My thoughts:

My affirmations for the day:

-
-
-

Today I am grateful for:

-
-
-
-
-

Access Journals &
More Self-Care Tools
On Our App

Scan to download!

How I feel right now:

 Amazing
 Good
 Okay
 Bad
 Terrible

My thoughts:

My affirmations for the day:

-
-
-

Today I am grateful for:

-
-
-
-
-

Access Affirmation
Cards & More Self-Care
Tools On Our App

Scan to download!

How I feel right now:

My thoughts:

My affirmations for the day:

-
-
-

Today I am grateful for:

-
-
-
-
-

Access Community &
More Self-Care Tools
On Our App

Scan to download!

__/__/____

Amazing

Good

Okay

Bad

Terrible

My thoughts:

All the effort is making a significant difference.

My affirmations for the day:

-
-
-

Today I am grateful for:

-
-
-
-
-

Access Breathing
Exercises & More
Self-Care Tools On Our

Scan to download!

__ / __ / ____

How I feel right now:

Amazing

Good

Okay

Bad

Terrible

My thoughts:

My affirmations for the day:

-
-
-

Today I am grateful for:

-
-
-
-
-

Access Affirmation
Cards & More Self-Care
Tools On Our App

Scan to download!

How I feel right now:

Amazing

Good

Okay

Bad

Terrible

My thoughts:

My affirmations for the day:

-
-
-

Today I am grateful for:

-
-
-
-
-

Access Community &
More Self-Care Tools
On Our App

Scan to download!

How I feel right now:

My thoughts:

My affirmations for the day:

- ....
- ....
- ....

Today I am grateful for:

- ....
- ....
- ....
- ....
- ....

Access Breathing
Exercises & More
Self-Care Tools On Our

Scan to download!

How I feel right now:

 Amazing

 Good

 Okay

 Bad

 Terrible

__ / __ / ____

My thoughts:

My affirmations for the day:

-
-
-

Today I am grateful for:

-
-
-
-
-

Access Journals &
More Self-Care Tools
On Our App

Scan to download!

How I feel right now:

My thoughts:

My affirmations for the day:

-
-
-

Today I am grateful for:

-
-
-
-
-

Access Affirmation Cards & More Self-Care Tools On Our App

Scan to download!

How I feel right now:

My thoughts:

My affirmations for the day:

-
-
-

Today I am grateful for:

-
-
-
-
-

Access Community &
More Self-Care Tools
On Our App

Scan to download!

How I feel right now:

Amazing

Good

Okay

Bad

Terrible

My thoughts:

....
....
....
....
....
....
....
....
....
....
....
....
....
....

My affirmations for the day:

- ....
- ....
- ....

Today I am grateful for:

- ....
- ....
- ....
- ....
- ....

Access Breathing
Exercises & More
Self-Care Tools On Our

Scan to download!

How I feel right now:

__/__/____

 Amazing

 Good

 Okay

 Bad

 Terrible

My thoughts:

My affirmations for the day:

-
-
-

Today I am grateful for:

-
-
-
-
-

Access Journals &
More Self-Care Tools
On Our App

Scan to download!

How I feel right now:

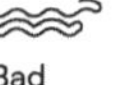

Amazing   Good   Okay   Bad   Terrible

My thoughts:

My affirmations for the day:

-
-
-

Today I am grateful for:

-
-
-
-
-

Access Affirmation Cards & More Self-Care Tools On Our App

Scan to download!

__/__/____

How I feel right now:

Amazing

Good

Okay

Bad

Terrible

My thoughts:

My affirmations for the day:

-
-
-

Today I am grateful for:

-
-
-
-
-

Access Community &
More Self-Care Tools
On Our App

Scan to download!

How I feel right now:

Amazing

Good

Okay

Bad

Terrible

My thoughts:

My affirmations for the day:

-
-
-

Today I am grateful for:

-
-
-
-
-

Access Breathing
Exercises & More
Self-Care Tools On Our

Scan to download!

How I feel right now:

Amazing

Good

Okay

Bad

Terrible

My thoughts:

My affirmations for the day:

-
-
-

Today I am grateful for:

-
-
-
-
-

Access Affirmation
Cards & More Self-Care
Tools On Our App

Scan to download!

__/__/____

How I feel right now:

 Amazing    Good    Okay    Bad    Terrible

My thoughts:

My affirmations for the day:

-
-
-

Today I am grateful for:

-
-
-
-
-

Access Community &
More Self-Care Tools
On Our App

Scan to download!

__ / __ / ____

My thoughts:

My affirmations for the day:

Today I am grateful for:

Access Breathing
Exercises & More
Self-Care Tools On Our

Scan to download!

 Amazing

 Good

 Okay

 Bad

 Terrible

My thoughts:

My affirmations for the day:

-
-
-

Today I am grateful for:

-
-
-
-
-

Access Journals &
More Self-Care Tools
On Our App

Scan to download!

How I feel right now:

My thoughts:

My affirmations for the day:

-
-
-

Today I am grateful for:

-
-
-
-
-

Access Affirmation Cards & More Self-Care Tools On Our App

Scan to download!

How I feel right now:

 Amazing  Good  Okay  Bad  Terrible

My thoughts:

My affirmations for the day:

-
-
-

Today I am grateful for:

-
-
-
-
-

Access Community &
More Self-Care Tools
On Our App

Scan to download!

How I feel right now:

Amazing

Good

Okay

Bad

Terrible

My thoughts:

Each step is a move closer to dreams, keep going!

My affirmations for the day:

-
-
-

Today I am grateful for:

-
-
-
-
-

Access Breathing
Exercises & More
Self-Care Tools On Our

Scan to download!

How I feel right now:

Amazing

Good

Okay

Bad

Terrible

My thoughts:

My affirmations for the day:

-
-
-

Today I am grateful for:

-
-
-
-
-

Access Journals &
More Self-Care Tools
On Our App

Scan to download!

__ / __ / ____

How I feel right now:

| Amazing | Good | Okay | Bad | Terrible |

My thoughts:

....
....
....
....
....
....
....
....
....
....
....
....
....
....

My affirmations for the day:

- ....
- ....
- ....

Today I am grateful for:

- ....
- ....
- ....
- ....
- ....

Access Affirmation
Cards & More Self-Care
Tools On Our App

Scan to download!

How I feel right now:

| Amazing | Good | Okay | Bad | Terrible |

My thoughts:

My affirmations for the day:

-
-
-

Today I am grateful for:

-
-
-
-
-

Access Community &
More Self-Care Tools
On Our App

Scan to download!

__ / __ / ____

My thoughts:

My affirmations for the day:

-
-
-

Today I am grateful for:

-
-
-
-
-

Access Breathing
Exercises & More
Self-Care Tools On Our

Scan to download!

How I feel right now:

| Amazing | Good | Okay | Bad | Terrible |

__/__/____

My thoughts:

My affirmations for the day:

- ....
- ....
- ....

Today I am grateful for:

- ....
- ....
- ....
- ....
- ....

Access Journals &
More Self-Care Tools
On Our App

Scan to download!

How I feel right now:

My thoughts:

My affirmations for the day:

-
-
-

Today I am grateful for:

-
-
-
-
-

Access Affirmation Cards & More Self-Care Tools On Our App

Scan to download!

My thoughts:

My affirmations for the day:

-
-
-

Today I am grateful for:

-
-
-
-
-

Access Community &
More Self-Care Tools
On Our App

Scan to download!

How I feel right now:

 Amazing

 Good

 Okay

 Bad

 Terrible

My thoughts:

My affirmations for the day:

- ....
- ....
- ....

Today I am grateful for:

- ....
- ....
- ....
- ....
- ....

Access Breathing
Exercises & More
Self-Care Tools On Our

Scan to download!

My thoughts:

My affirmations for the day:

-
-
-

Today I am grateful for:

-
-
-
-
-

Access Journals &
More Self-Care Tools
On Our App

Scan to download!

How I feel right now:

Amazing	Good	Okay	Bad	Terrible

My thoughts:

My affirmations for the day:

-
-
-

Today I am grateful for:

-
-
-
-
-

Access Affirmation Cards & More Self-Care Tools On Our App

Scan to download!

My thoughts:

My affirmations for the day:

-
-
-

Today I am grateful for:

-
-
-
-
-

Access Community &
More Self-Care Tools
On Our App

Scan to download!

How I feel right now:

My thoughts:

My affirmations for the day:

-
-
-

Today I am grateful for:

-
-
-
-
-

Access Breathing
Exercises & More
Self-Care Tools On Our

Scan to download!

How I feel right now:

__ / __ / ____

Amazing

Good

Okay

Bad

Terrible

My thoughts:

My affirmations for the day:

-
-
-

Today I am grateful for:

-
-
-
-
-

Access Journals &
More Self-Care Tools
On Our App

Scan to download!

How I feel right now:

My thoughts:

My affirmations for the day:

-
-
-

Today I am grateful for:

-
-
-
-
-

Access Affirmation Cards & More Self-Care Tools On Our App

Scan to download!

__ / __ / ____

How I feel right now:

| Amazing | Good | Okay | Bad | Terrible |

My thoughts:

My affirmations for the day:

- ....
- ....
- ....

Today I am grateful for:

- ....
- ....
- ....
- ....
- ....

Access Community &
More Self-Care Tools
On Our App

Scan to download!

__ / __ / ____

How I feel right now:

Amazing

Good

Okay

Bad

Terrible

My thoughts:

My affirmations for the day:

-
-
-

Today I am grateful for:

-
-
-
-
-

Access Breathing
Exercises & More
Self-Care Tools On Our

Scan to download!

How I feel right now:

My thoughts:

My affirmations for the day:

-
-
-

Today I am grateful for:

-
-
-
-
-

Access Journals &
More Self-Care Tools
On Our App

Scan to download!

How I feel right now:

Amazing

Good

Okay

Bad

Terrible

My thoughts:

My affirmations for the day:

-
-
-

Today I am grateful for:

-
-
-
-
-

Access Affirmation
Cards & More Self-Care
Tools On Our App

Scan to download!

How I feel right now:

Amazing · Good · Okay · Bad · Terrible

My thoughts:

My affirmations for the day:

- ....
- ....
- ....

Today I am grateful for:

- ....
- ....
- ....
- ....
- ....

Access Community &
More Self-Care Tools
On Our App

Scan to download!

How I feel right now:

| Amazing | Good | Okay | Bad | Terrible |

My thoughts:

Progress is visible, aim for the stars!

My affirmations for the day:

-
-
-

Today I am grateful for:

-
-
-
-
-

Access Breathing
Exercises & More
Self-Care Tools On Our

Scan to download!

How I feel right now:

Amazing

Good

Okay

Bad

Terrible

My thoughts:

My affirmations for the day:

-
-
-

Today I am grateful for:

-
-
-
-
-

Access Journals &
More Self-Care Tools
On Our App

Scan to download!

__ / __ / ____

How I feel right now:

 Amazing

 Good

 Okay

 Bad

 Terrible

My thoughts:

My affirmations for the day:

-
-
-

Today I am grateful for:

-
-
-
-
-

Scan to download!

How I feel right now:

My thoughts:

My affirmations for the day:

-
-
-

Today I am grateful for:

-
-
-
-
-

Access Community &
More Self-Care Tools
On Our App

Scan to download!

How I feel right now:

My thoughts:

My affirmations for the day:

-
-
-

Today I am grateful for:

-
-
-
-
-

Access Breathing
Exercises & More
Self-Care Tools On Our

Scan to download!

How I feel right now:

__/__/____

Amazing

Good

Okay

Bad

Terrible

My thoughts:

My affirmations for the day:

-
-
-

Today I am grateful for:

-
-
-
-
-

Access Journals &
More Self-Care Tools
On Our App

Scan to download!

How I feel right now:

_ _ / _ _ / _ _ _ _

 Amazing    Good    Okay    Bad    Terrible

My thoughts:

....
....
....
....
....
....
....
....
....
....
....
....
....
....
....

My affirmations for the day:

- ....
- ....
- ....

Today I am grateful for:

- ....
- ....
- ....
- ....
- ....

Access Affirmation Cards & More Self-Care Tools On Our App

Scan to download!

My thoughts:

My affirmations for the day:

-
-
-

Today I am grateful for:

-
-
-
-
-

Access Community &
More Self-Care Tools
On Our App

Scan to download!

How I feel right now:

 Amazing
 Good
 Okay
 Bad
 Terrible

My thoughts:

My affirmations for the day:

-
-
-

Today I am grateful for:

-
-
-
-
-

Access Breathing
Exercises & More
Self-Care Tools On Our

Scan to download!

How I feel right now:

Amazing

Good

Okay

Bad

Terrible

My thoughts:

My affirmations for the day:

-
-
-

Today I am grateful for:

-
-
-
-
-

Access Journals &
More Self-Care Tools
On Our App

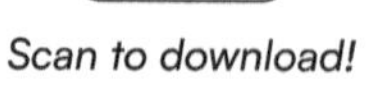

Scan to download!

How I feel right now:

My thoughts:

My affirmations for the day:

-
-
-

Today I am grateful for:

-
-
-
-
-

Access Affirmation Cards & More Self-Care Tools On Our App

Scan to download!

How I feel right now:

Amazing

Good

Okay

Bad

Terrible

My thoughts:

My affirmations for the day:

-
-
-

Today I am grateful for:

-
-
-
-
-

Access Community &
More Self-Care Tools
On Our App

Scan to download!

How I feel right now:

__ / __ / ____

Amazing   Good   Okay   Bad   Terrible

My thoughts:

My affirmations for the day:

-
-
-

Today I am grateful for:

-
-
-
-
-

Access Breathing
Exercises & More
Self-Care Tools On Our

Scan to download!

How I feel right now:

Amazing

Good

Okay

Bad

Terrible

My thoughts:

My affirmations for the day:

-
-
-

Today I am grateful for:

-
-
-
-
-

Access Journals &
More Self-Care Tools
On Our App

Scan to download!

How I feel right now:

__ / __ / ____

 Amazing    Good    Okay    Bad    Terrible

My thoughts:

My affirmations for the day:

-
-
-

Today I am grateful for:

-
-
-
-
-

Access Affirmation
Cards & More Self-Care
Tools On Our App

Scan to download!

How I feel right now:

__/__/____

Amazing

Good

Okay

Bad

Terrible

My thoughts:

My affirmations for the day:

-
-
-

Today I am grateful for:

-
-
-
-
-

Access Community &
More Self-Care Tools
On Our App

Scan to download!

How I feel right now:

__ __ / __ __ / __ __ __ __

Amazing

Good

Okay

Bad

Terrible

My thoughts:

My affirmations for the day:

-
-
-

Today I am grateful for:

-
-
-
-
-

Access Breathing
Exercises & More
Self-Care Tools On Our

Scan to download!

_ _ / _ _ / _ _ _ _

How I feel right now:

Amazing

Good

Okay

Bad

Terrible

My thoughts:

My affirmations for the day:

- ....
- ....
- ....

Today I am grateful for:

- ....
- ....
- ....
- ....
- ....

Access Journals &
More Self-Care Tools
On Our App

Scan to download!

How I feel right now:

 Amazing

 Good

 Okay

 Bad

 Terrible

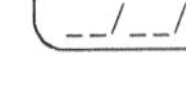

My thoughts:

My affirmations for the day:

- ....
- ....
- ....

Today I am grateful for:

- ....
- ....
- ....
- ....
- ....

Access Affirmation
Cards & More Self-Care
Tools On Our App

Scan to download!

__/__/____

How I feel right now:

Amazing   Good   Okay   Bad   Terrible

My thoughts:

My affirmations for the day:

-
-
-

Today I am grateful for:

-
-
-
-
-

Access Community &
More Self-Care Tools
On Our App

Scan to download!

How I feel right now:

Amazing	Good	Okay	Bad	Terrible

My thoughts:

100 days of self-love & dedication- an impressive milestone

My affirmations for the day:

-
-
-

Today I am grateful for:

-
-
-
-
-

Access Breathing
Exercises & More
Self-Care Tools On Our

Scan to download!

How I feel right now:

__/__/____

Amazing

Good

Okay

Bad

Terrible

My thoughts:

My affirmations for the day:

-
-
-

Today I am grateful for:

-
-
-
-
-

Access Journals &
More Self-Care Tools
On Our App

Scan to download!

How I feel right now:

__ / __ / ____

My thoughts:

My affirmations for the day:

-
-
-

Today I am grateful for:

-
-
-
-
-

Access Affirmation Cards & More Self-Care Tools On Our App

Scan to download!

__/__/____

How I feel right now:

| Amazing | Good | Okay | Bad | Terrible |

My thoughts:

My affirmations for the day:

-
-
-

Today I am grateful for:

-
-
-
-
-

How I feel right now:

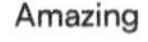

Amazing   Good   Okay   Bad   Terrible

My thoughts:

My affirmations for the day:

- ....
- ....
- ....

Today I am grateful for:

- ....
- ....
- ....
- ....
- ....

Access Breathing
Exercises & More
Self-Care Tools On Our

Scan to download!

How I feel right now:

My thoughts:

My affirmations for the day:

Today I am grateful for:

Access Journals &
More Self-Care Tools
On Our App

Scan to download!

How I feel right now:

Amazing

Good

Okay

Bad

Terrible

My thoughts:

My affirmations for the day:

- ....
- ....
- ....

Today I am grateful for:

- ....
- ....
- ....
- ....
- ....

Access Affirmation
Cards & More Self-Care
Tools On Our App

Scan to download!

How I feel right now:

My thoughts:

My affirmations for the day:

-
-
-

Today I am grateful for:

-
-
-
-
-

Access Breathing
Exercises & More
Self-Care Tools On Our

Scan to download!

How I feel right now:

__/__/____

Amazing

Good

Okay

Bad

Terrible

My thoughts:

My affirmations for the day:

-
-
-

Today I am grateful for:

-
-
-
-
-

Access Journals &
More Self-Care Tools
On Our App

Scan to download!

How I feel right now:

__/__/____

| Amazing | Good | Okay | Bad | Terrible |

My thoughts:

My affirmations for the day:

-
-
-

Today I am grateful for:

-
-
-
-
-

Access Affirmation
Cards & More Self-Care
Tools On Our App

Scan to download!

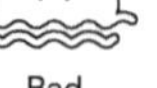

My thoughts:

My affirmations for the day:

-
-
-

Today I am grateful for:

-
-
-
-
-

Access Community &
More Self-Care Tools
On Our App

Scan to download!

How I feel right now:

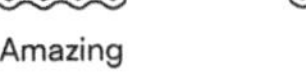

Amazing

Good

Okay

Bad

Terrible

My thoughts:

My affirmations for the day:

-
-
-

Today I am grateful for:

-
-
-
-
-

Access Breathing
Exercises & More
Self-Care Tools On Our

Scan to download!

How I feel right now:

Amazing

Good

Okay

Bad

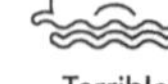
Terrible

My thoughts:

My affirmations for the day:

-
-
-

Today I am grateful for:

-
-
-
-
-

Access Journals &
More Self-Care Tools
On Our App

Scan to download!

__ / __ / ____

How I feel right now:

 Amazing
 Good
 Okay
 Bad
 Terrible

My thoughts:

My affirmations for the day:

-
-
-

Today I am grateful for:

-
-
-
-
-

Access Affirmation Cards & More Self-Care Tools On Our App

Scan to download!

How I feel right now:

 Amazing
 Good
 Okay
 Bad
 Terrible

My thoughts:

My affirmations for the day:

-
-
-

Today I am grateful for:

-
-
-
-
-

Access Community &
More Self-Care Tools
On Our App

Scan to download!

How I feel right now:

| Amazing | Good | Okay | Bad | Terrible |

My thoughts:

My affirmations for the day:

-
-
-

Today I am grateful for:

-
-
-
-
-

Access Breathing
Exercises & More
Self-Care Tools On Our

Scan to download!

How I feel right now:

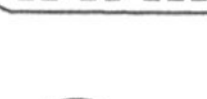

| Amazing | Good | Okay | Bad | Terrible |

My thoughts:

....
....
....
....
....
....
....
....
....
....
....
....
....
....

My affirmations for the day:

- ....
- ....
- ....

Today I am grateful for:

- ....
- ....
- ....
- ....
- ....

Access Journals &
More Self-Care Tools
On Our App

Scan to download!

How I feel right now:

__/__/____

| Amazing | Good | Okay | Bad | Terrible |

My thoughts:

My affirmations for the day:

-
-
-

Today I am grateful for:

-
-
-
-
-

Access Affirmation
Cards & More Self-Care
Tools On Our App

Scan to download!

| How I feel right now: | __/__/____ |

Amazing

Good

Okay

Bad

Terrible

My thoughts:

My affirmations for the day:

-
-
-

Today I am grateful for:

-
-
-
-
-

Access Community &
More Self-Care Tools
On Our App

Scan to download!

How I feel right now:

My thoughts:

Consistency reflects determination. Greatness is within reach, keep moving confidently!

My affirmations for the day:

-
-
-

Today I am grateful for:

-
-
-
-
-

Access Breathing
Exercises & More
Self-Care Tools On Our

Scan to download!

How I feel right now:

Amazing

Good

Okay

Bad

Terrible

My thoughts:

My affirmations for the day:

-
-
-

Today I am grateful for:

-
-
-
-
-

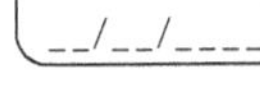

How I feel right now:

Amazing

Good

Okay

Bad

Terrible

My thoughts:

My affirmations for the day:

- ......
- ......
- ......

Today I am grateful for:

- ......
- ......
- ......
- ......
- ......

Access Affirmation Cards & More Self-Care Tools On Our App

Scan to download!

How I feel right now:

 Amazing

 Good

 Okay

 Bad

 Terrible

My thoughts:

....
....
....
....
....
....
....
....
....
....
....
....
....
....

My affirmations for the day:

- ....
- ....
- ....

Today I am grateful for:

- ....
- ....
- ....
- ....
- ....

Access Community &
More Self-Care Tools
On Our App

Scan to download!

How I feel right now:

My thoughts:

My affirmations for the day:

-
-
-

Today I am grateful for:

-
-
-
-
-

Access Breathing
Exercises & More
Self-Care Tools On Our

Scan to download!

How I feel right now:

My thoughts:

My affirmations for the day:

-
-
-

Today I am grateful for:

-
-
-
-
-

Access Journals &
More Self-Care Tools
On Our App

Scan to download!

How I feel right now:

My thoughts:

My affirmations for the day:

-
-
-

Today I am grateful for:

-
-
-
-
-

Access Affirmation
Cards & More Self-Care
Tools On Our App

Scan to download!

How I feel right now: __/__/____

Amazing   Good   Okay   Bad   Terrible

My thoughts:

....
....
....
....
....
....
....
....
....
....
....
....
....
....

My affirmations for the day:

- ....
- ....
- ....

Today I am grateful for:

- ....
- ....
- ....
- ....
- ....

Access Community &
More Self-Care Tools
On Our App

Scan to download!

__/__/____

How I feel right now:

| Amazing | Good | Okay | Bad | Terrible |

My thoughts:

My affirmations for the day:

-
-
-

Today I am grateful for:

-
-
-
-
-

Access Breathing
Exercises & More
Self-Care Tools On Our

Scan to download!

__ / __ / ____

How I feel right now:

 Amazing

 Good

 Okay

 Bad

 Terrible

My thoughts:

My affirmations for the day:

-
-
-

Today I am grateful for:

-
-
-
-
-

Access Journals &
More Self-Care Tools
On Our App

Scan to download!

How I feel right now:

Amazing

Good

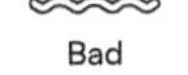
Okay

Bad

Terrible

My thoughts:

My affirmations for the day:

-
-
-

Today I am grateful for:

-
-
-
-
-

Access Affirmation
Cards & More Self-Care
Tools On Our App

Scan to download!

How I feel right now:

Amazing

Good

Okay

Bad

Terrible

My thoughts:

My affirmations for the day:

- ....
- ....
- ....

Today I am grateful for:

- ....
- ....
- ....
- ....
- ....

Access Community &
More Self-Care Tools
On Our App

Scan to download!

How I feel right now:

__ /__ /____

Amazing

Good

Okay

Bad

Terrible

My thoughts:

My affirmations for the day:

-
-
-

Today I am grateful for:

-
-
-
-
-

Access Breathing
Exercises & More
Self-Care Tools On Our

Scan to download!

How I feel right now:

__ / __ / ____

Amazing

Good

Okay

Bad

Terrible

My thoughts:

My affirmations for the day:

-
-
-

Today I am grateful for:

-
-
-
-
-

Access Journals &
More Self-Care Tools
On Our App

Scan to download!

How I feel right now:

Amazing   Good   Okay   Bad   Terrible

My thoughts:

My affirmations for the day:

-
-
-

Today I am grateful for:

-
-
-
-
-

Access Affirmation
Cards & More Self-Care
Tools On Our App

Scan to download!

How I feel right now:

 Amazing
 Good
 Okay
 Bad
 Terrible

My thoughts:

My affirmations for the day:

-
-
-

Today I am grateful for:

-
-
-
-
-

Access Community &
More Self-Care Tools
On Our App

Scan to download!

How I feel right now:

My thoughts:

My affirmations for the day:

-
-
-

Today I am grateful for:

-
-
-
-
-

Access Breathing
Exercises & More
Self-Care Tools On Our

Scan to download!

__/__/____

How I feel right now:

Amazing

Good

Okay

Bad

Terrible

My thoughts:

My affirmations for the day:

-
-
-

Today I am grateful for:

-
-
-
-
-

Access Journals &
More Self-Care Tools
On Our App

Scan to download!

How I feel right now:

 Amazing
 Good
Okay
 Bad
 Terrible

My thoughts:

My affirmations for the day:

-
-
-

Today I am grateful for:

-
-
-
-
-

Access Affirmation
Cards & More Self-Care
Tools On Our App

Scan to download!

__ / __ / ____

My thoughts:

My affirmations for the day:

-
-
-

Today I am grateful for:

-
-
-
-
-

Access Community &
More Self-Care Tools
On Our App

Scan to download!

How I feel right now:

Amazing

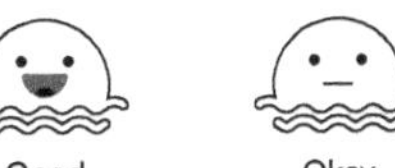
Good

Okay

Bad

Terrible

My thoughts:

....
....
....
....
....
....
....
....
....
....
....
....
....

Every step forward is a victory, celebrate the progress!

My affirmations for the day:

- ....
- ....
- ....

Today I am grateful for:

- ....
- ....
- ....
- ....
- ....

Access Breathing
Exercises & More
Self-Care Tools On Our

Scan to download!

How I feel right now:

My thoughts:

My affirmations for the day:

-
-
-

Today I am grateful for:

-
-
-
-
-

Access Journals &
More Self-Care Tools
On Our App

Scan to download!

How I feel right now:

Okay

Bad

My thoughts:

My affirmations for the day:

-
-
-

Today I am grateful for:

-
-
-
-
-

Access Affirmation
Cards & More Self-Care
Tools On Our App

Scan to download!

How I feel right now:

Amazing	Good	Okay	Bad	Terrible

My thoughts:

My affirmations for the day:

-
-
-

Today I am grateful for:

-
-
-
-
-

Access Community &
More Self-Care Tools
On Our App

Scan to download!

How I feel right now:

__ / __ / ____

 Amazing

 Good

Okay

 Bad

 Terrible

My thoughts:

My affirmations for the day:

-
-
-

Today I am grateful for:

-
-
-
-
-

Access Breathing
Exercises & More
Self-Care Tools On Our

Scan to download!

How I feel right now:

Amazing

Good

Okay

Bad

Terrible

My thoughts:

My affirmations for the day:

-
-
-

Today I am grateful for:

-
-
-
-
-

Access Journals &
More Self-Care Tools
On Our App

Scan to download!

How I feel right now:

Amazing   Good   Okay   Bad   Terrible

My thoughts:

My affirmations for the day:

- ....
- ....
- ....

Today I am grateful for:

- ....
- ....
- ....
- ....
- ....

Access Affirmation
Cards & More Self-Care
Tools On Our App

Scan to download!

How I feel right now:

 Amazing  Good  Okay  Bad  Terrible

My thoughts:

My affirmations for the day:

-
-
-

Today I am grateful for:

-
-
-
-
-

Access Community &
More Self-Care Tools
On Our App

Scan to download!

How I feel right now:

Amazing

Good

Okay

Bad

Terrible

My thoughts:

My affirmations for the day:

-
-
-

Today I am grateful for:

-
-
-
-
-

Access Breathing
Exercises & More
Self-Care Tools On Our

Scan to download!

How I feel right now:

 Amazing
 Good
 Okay
 Bad
 Terrible

My thoughts:

My affirmations for the day:

-
-
-

Today I am grateful for:

-
-
-
-
-

Access Journals &
More Self-Care Tools
On Our App

Scan to download!

_ _ / _ _ / _ _ _ _

How I feel right now:

Amazing

Good

Okay

Bad

Terrible

My thoughts:

My affirmations for the day:

- ....
- ....
- ....

Today I am grateful for:

- ....
- ....
- ....
- ....
- ....

Access Affirmation Cards & More Self-Care Tools On Our App

Scan to download!

How I feel right now:

 Amazing
 Good
 Okay
 Bad
 Terrible

__ / __ / ____

My thoughts:

My affirmations for the day:

-
-
-

Today I am grateful for:

-
-
-
-
-

Access Community &
More Self-Care Tools
On Our App

Scan to download!

How I feel right now:

__/__/____

 Amazing

 Good

 Okay

 Bad

 Terrible

---

My thoughts:

....
....
....
....
....
....
....
....
....
....
....
....
....
....
....
....

My affirmations for the day:

- ....
- ....
- ....

Today I am grateful for:

- ....
- ....
- ....
- ....
- ....

Access Breathing
Exercises & More
Self-Care Tools On Our

Scan to download!

How I feel right now:

__/__/____

My thoughts:

My affirmations for the day:

-
-
-

Today I am grateful for:

-
-
-
-
-

Access Journals &
More Self-Care Tools
On Our App

Scan to download!

How I feel right now:

Amazing

Good

Okay

Bad

Terrible

My thoughts:

My affirmations for the day:

-
-
-

Today I am grateful for:

-
-
-
-
-

Access Affirmation
Cards & More Self-Care
Tools On Our App

Scan to download!

How I feel right now:

__/__/____

Amazing

Good

Okay

Bad

Terrible

My thoughts:

My affirmations for the day:

-
-
-

Today I am grateful for:

-
-
-
-
-

Access Community &
More Self-Care Tools
On Our App

Scan to download!

My thoughts:

My affirmations for the day:

Today I am grateful for:

Access Journals &
More Self-Care Tools
On Our App

Scan to download!

How I feel right now:

Amazing   Good   Okay   Bad   Terrible

My thoughts:

My affirmations for the day:

-
-
-

Today I am grateful for:

-
-
-
-
-

Access Affirmation
Cards & More Self-Care
Tools On Our App

Scan to download!

How I feel right now:

 Amazing

 Good

 Okay

 Bad

 Terrible

My thoughts:

My affirmations for the day:

-
-
-

Today I am grateful for:

-
-
-
-
-

Access Community &
More Self-Care Tools
On Our App

Scan to download!

__ / __ / ____

My thoughts:

*This journey shows strength, keep going,
the best is yet to come!*

My affirmations for the day:

-
-
-

Today I am grateful for:

-
-
-
-
-

Access Breathing
Exercises & More
Self-Care Tools On Our

Scan to download!

How I feel right now:

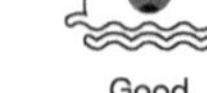

My thoughts:

My affirmations for the day:

-
-
-

Today I am grateful for:

-
-
-
-
-

Access Journals &
More Self-Care Tools
On Our App

Scan to download!

How I feel right now:

__ / __ / ____

Amazing   Good   Okay   Bad   Terrible

My thoughts:

My affirmations for the day:

-
-
-

Today I am grateful for:

-
-
-
-
-

Access Affirmation Cards & More Self-Care Tools On Our App

Scan to download!

How I feel right now:

| Amazing | Good | Okay | Bad | Terrible |

My thoughts:

My affirmations for the day:

-
-
-

Today I am grateful for:

-
-
-
-
-

Access Community &
More Self-Care Tools
On Our App

Scan to download!

How I feel right now:

Amazing

Good

Okay

Bad

Terrible

My thoughts:

My affirmations for the day:

-
-
-

Today I am grateful for:

-
-
-
-
-

Access Breathing
Exercises & More
Self-Care Tools On Our

Scan to download!

How I feel right now:

My thoughts:

My affirmations for the day:

-
-
-

Today I am grateful for:

-
-
-
-
-

Access Journals &
More Self-Care Tools
On Our App

Scan to download!

My thoughts:

My affirmations for the day:

- ....
- ....
- ....

Today I am grateful for:

- ....
- ....
- ....
- ....
- ....

Access Affirmation
Cards & More Self-Care
Tools On Our App

Scan to download!

How I feel right now:

My thoughts:

My affirmations for the day:

-
-
-

Today I am grateful for:

-
-
-
-
-

Access Community &
More Self-Care Tools
On Our App

Scan to download!

My thoughts:

My affirmations for the day:

-
-
-

Today I am grateful for:

-
-
-
-
-

Access Breathing
Exercises & More
Self-Care Tools On Our

Scan to download!

__ / __ / ____

How I feel right now:

Amazing

Good

Okay

Bad

Terrible

My thoughts:

....
....
....
....
....
....
....
....
....
....
....
....
....
....

My affirmations for the day:

- ....
- ....
- ....

Today I am grateful for:

- ....
- ....
- ....
- ....
- ....

Access Journals &
More Self-Care Tools
On Our App

Scan to download!

How I feel right now:

Amazing

Good

Okay

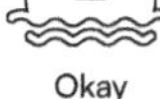

Bad

Terrible

__/__/____

My thoughts:

My affirmations for the day:

-
-
-

Today I am grateful for:

-
-
-
-
-

Access Affirmation
Cards & More Self-Care
Tools On Our App

Scan to download!

How I feel right now:

Amazing

Good

Okay

Bad

Terrible

My thoughts:

My affirmations for the day:

- ....
- ....
- ....

Today I am grateful for:

- ....
- ....
- ....
- ....
- ....

Access Community &
More Self-Care Tools
On Our App

Scan to download!

How I feel right now:

Amazing

Good

Okay

Bad

Terrible

My thoughts:

My affirmations for the day:

- ....
- ....
- ....

Today I am grateful for:

- ....
- ....
- ....
- ....
- ....

Access Breathing
Exercises & More
Self-Care Tools On Our

Scan to download!

How I feel right now:

__ / __ / ____

 Amazing  Good  Okay  Bad  Terrible

My thoughts:

My affirmations for the day:

-
-
-

Today I am grateful for:

-
-
-
-
-

Access Journals &
More Self-Care Tools
On Our App

Scan to download!

How I feel right now:

My thoughts:

My affirmations for the day:

-
-
-

Today I am grateful for:

-
-
-
-
-

Access Affirmation Cards & More Self-Care Tools On Our App

Scan to download!

How I feel right now:

My thoughts:

My affirmations for the day:

-
-
-

Today I am grateful for:

-
-
-
-
-

Access Community &
More Self-Care Tools
On Our App

Scan to download!

How I feel right now:

  Amazing

 Good

 Okay

 Bad

 Terrible

My thoughts:

My affirmations for the day:

-
-
-

Today I am grateful for:

-
-
-
-
-

How I feel right now:

Amazing

Good

Okay

Bad

Terrible

My thoughts:

My affirmations for the day:

-
-
-

Today I am grateful for:

-
-
-
-
-

Access Journals &
More Self-Care Tools
On Our App

Scan to download!

How I feel right now:

Amazing

Good

Okay

Bad

Terrible

My thoughts:

My affirmations for the day:

-
-
-

Today I am grateful for:

-
-
-
-
-

Access Affirmation
Cards & More Self-Care
Tools On Our App

Scan to download!

How I feel right now:

 Amazing

 Good

 Okay

 Bad

 Terrible

My thoughts:

My affirmations for the day:

-
-
-

Today I am grateful for:

-
-
-
-
-

Access Community &
More Self-Care Tools
On Our App

Scan to download!

How I feel right now:

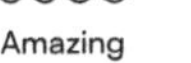
Amazing

Good

Okay

Bad

Terrible

My thoughts:

Discipline reflects self-love, well-deserved pride!

My affirmations for the day:

-
-
-

Today I am grateful for:

-
-
-
-
-

Access Breathing
Exercises & More
Self-Care Tools On Our

Scan to download!

My thoughts:

My affirmations for the day:

Today I am grateful for:

Access Journals &
More Self-Care Tools
On Our App

Scan to download!

How I feel right now:

My thoughts:

My affirmations for the day:

-
-
-

Today I am grateful for:

-
-
-
-
-

Access Affirmation Cards & More Self-Care Tools On Our App

Scan to download!

__/__/____

How I feel right now:

My thoughts:

My affirmations for the day:

-
-
-

Today I am grateful for:

-
-
-
-
-

Access Community &
More Self-Care Tools
On Our App

Scan to download!

How I feel right now:

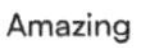
Amazing

Good

Okay

Bad

Terrible

My thoughts:

My affirmations for the day:

-
-
-

Today I am grateful for:

-
-
-
-
-

Access Breathing
Exercises & More
Self-Care Tools On Our

Scan to download!

How I feel right now:

__ / __ / ____

Amazing   Good   Okay   Bad   Terrible

My thoughts:

My affirmations for the day:

-
-
-

Today I am grateful for:

-
-
-
-
-

Access Affirmation
Cards & More Self-Care
Tools On Our App

Scan to download!

How I feel right now:

Amazing	Good	Okay	Bad	Terrible

My thoughts:

My affirmations for the day:

-
-
-

Today I am grateful for:

-
-
-
-
-

Access Community &
More Self-Care Tools
On Our App

Scan to download!

How I feel right now:

My thoughts:

My affirmations for the day:

-
-
-

Today I am grateful for:

-
-
-
-
-

Access Breathing
Exercises & More
Self-Care Tools On Our

Scan to download!

How I feel right now:

 Amazing

 Good

 Okay

Bad

 Terrible

My thoughts:

My affirmations for the day:

-
-
-

Today I am grateful for:

-
-
-
-
-

Access Journals &
More Self-Care Tools
On Our App

Scan to download!

How I feel right now:

| Amazing | Good | Okay | Bad | Terrible |

My thoughts:

My affirmations for the day:

-
-
-

Today I am grateful for:

-
-
-
-
-

Access Affirmation
Cards & More Self-Care
Tools On Our App

Scan to download!

How I feel right now:

 Amazing
 Good
 Okay
 Bad
 Terrible

My thoughts:

My affirmations for the day:

-
-
-

Today I am grateful for:

-
-
-
-
-

Access Community &
More Self-Care Tools
On Our App

Scan to download!

How I feel right now:

Amazing

Good

Okay

Bad

Terrible

My thoughts:

My affirmations for the day:

- ....
- ....
- ....

Today I am grateful for:

- ....
- ....
- ....
- ....
- ....

Access Breathing
Exercises & More
Self-Care Tools On Our

Scan to download!

How I feel right now:

| Amazing | Good | Okay | Bad | Terrible |

My thoughts:

My affirmations for the day:

- ....
- ....
- ....

Today I am grateful for:

- ....
- ....
- ....
- ....
- ....

Access Journals &
More Self-Care Tools
On Our App

Scan to download!

How I feel right now:

My thoughts:

My affirmations for the day:

-
-
-

Today I am grateful for:

-
-
-
-
-

Access Affirmation
Cards & More Self-Care
Tools On Our App

Scan to download!

How I feel right now:

| Amazing | Good | Okay | Bad | Terrible |

My thoughts:

My affirmations for the day:

-
-
-

Today I am grateful for:

-
-
-
-
-

Access Community &
More Self-Care Tools
On Our App

Scan to download!

How I feel right now:

Amazing   Good   Okay   Bad   Terrible

My thoughts:

Congratulations on the accomplishment,
196 days of discipline, a proud moment!

My affirmations for the day:

-
-
-

Today I am grateful for:

-
-
-
-
-

Access Breathing
Exercises & More
Self-Care Tools On Our

Scan to download!

Congratulations! You've reached the end of an epic journey!

For *196 days,* you've dedicated yourself to self-care, growth, and reflection. This is a truly impressive milestone, and your progress makes us so proud.

Take a moment to celebrate your consistency, dedication and growth!

Enjoyed this journey? **Keep exploring & progress ahead in the next journal!**

Download the Mind Alcove app to access more self-care tools!

www.ingramcontent.com/pod-product-compliance
Lightning Source LLC
Chambersburg PA
CBHW041314120726

48005CB00014B/2002